No, David!

By

David Shannon

SCHOLASTIC INC.
New York Toronto London Auckland Sydney
Mexico City New Delhi Hong Kong

To Martha, my mother, who kept me in line then,
and to Heidi, my wife, who keeps me in line now.

AUTHOR'S NOTE

A few years ago, my mother sent me a book
I made when I was a little boy. It was called
No, David, and it was illustrated with drawings of
David doing all sorts of things he wasn't supposed
to do. The text consisted entirely of the words "no"
and "David." (They were the only words I knew
how to spell.) I thought it would be fun to do a
remake celebrating those familiar variations of the
universal "no" that we all hear while growing up.

    Of course, "yes" is a wonderful word. . .but "yes"
doesn't keep crayon off the living room wall.

This book was originally published in hardcover by the Blue Sky Press in 1998.

ISBN 0-439-12965-6

12 11 10 9 8 7 6 5 4 3 2 1   9/9 0 1 2 3 4/0

Printed in Mexico   49

First Scholastic club printing, September 1999

David's mom always said...

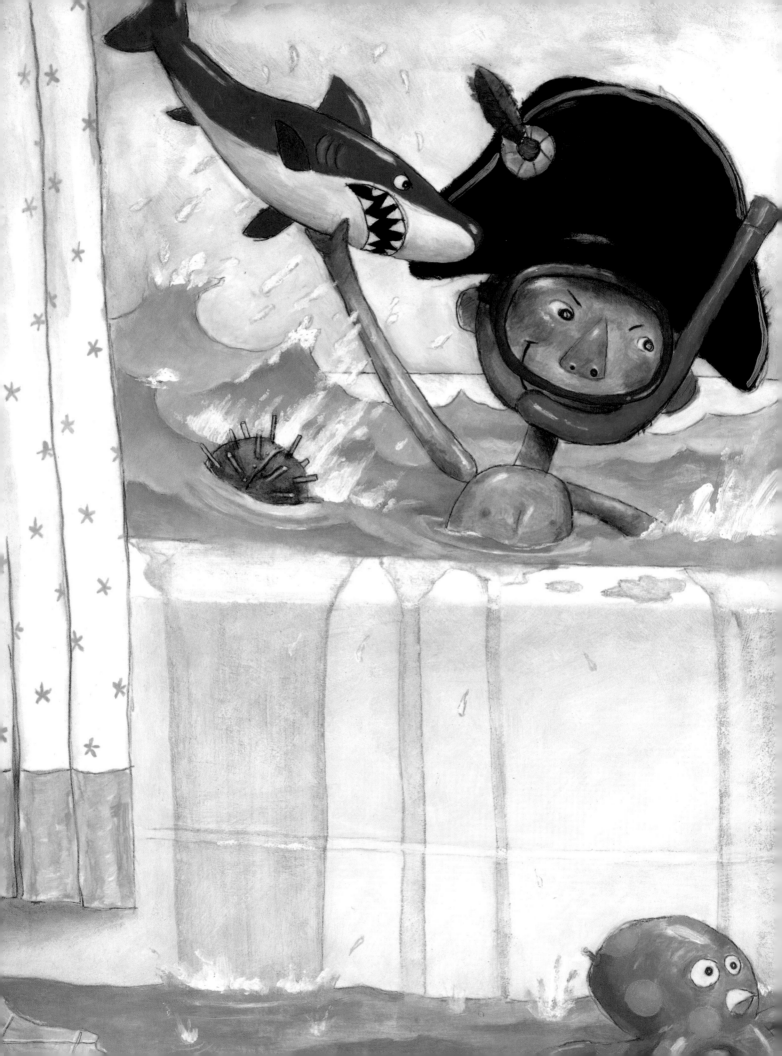

here, David !

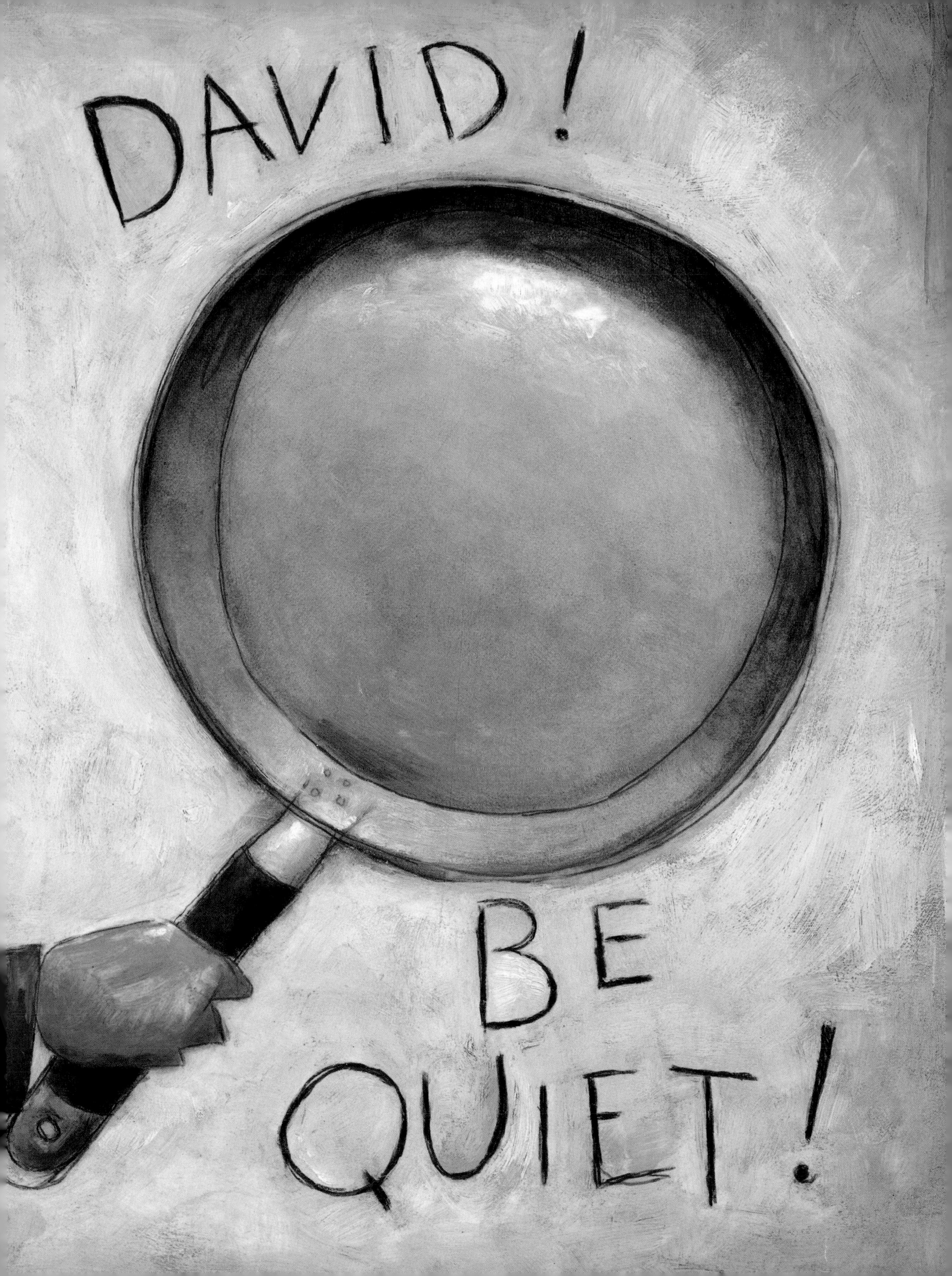
DAVID!
BE QUIET!

That's enough,

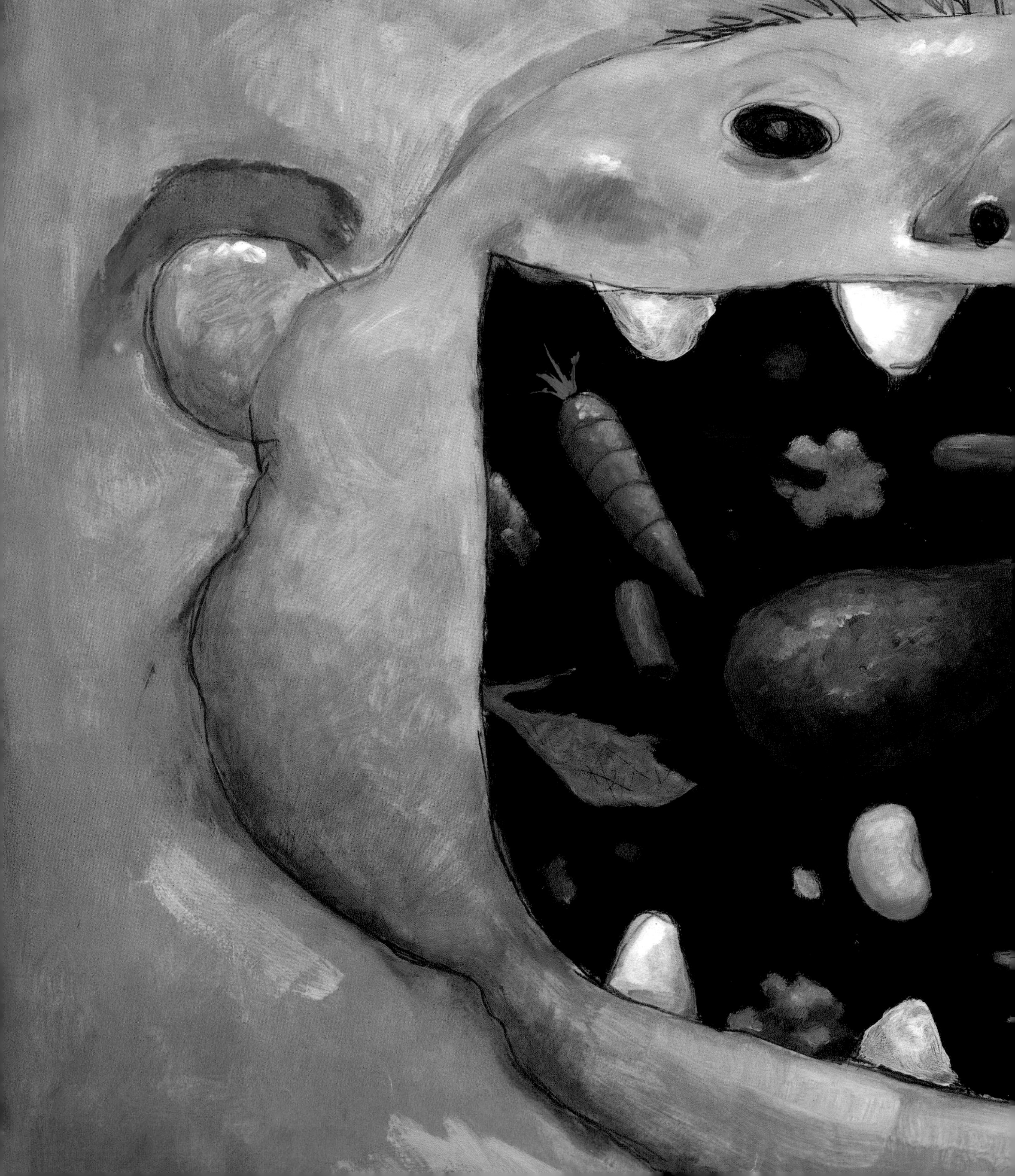

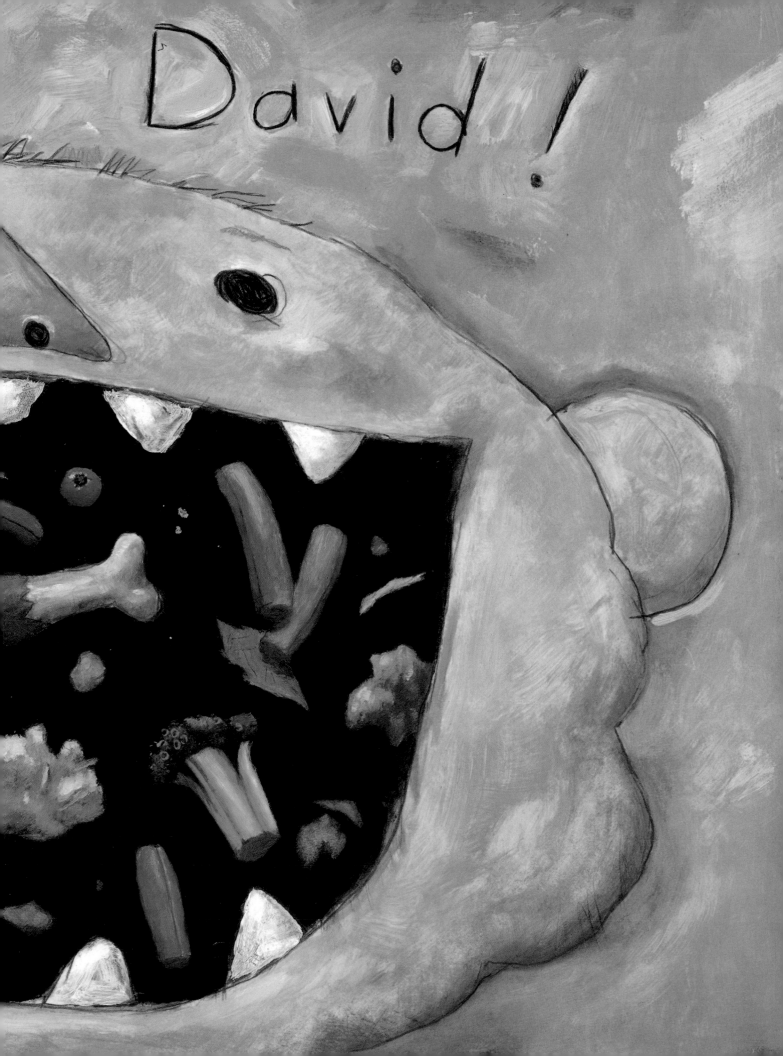

Go to

your   room!

Put your toys away!

Not in the

house, David!

come here.

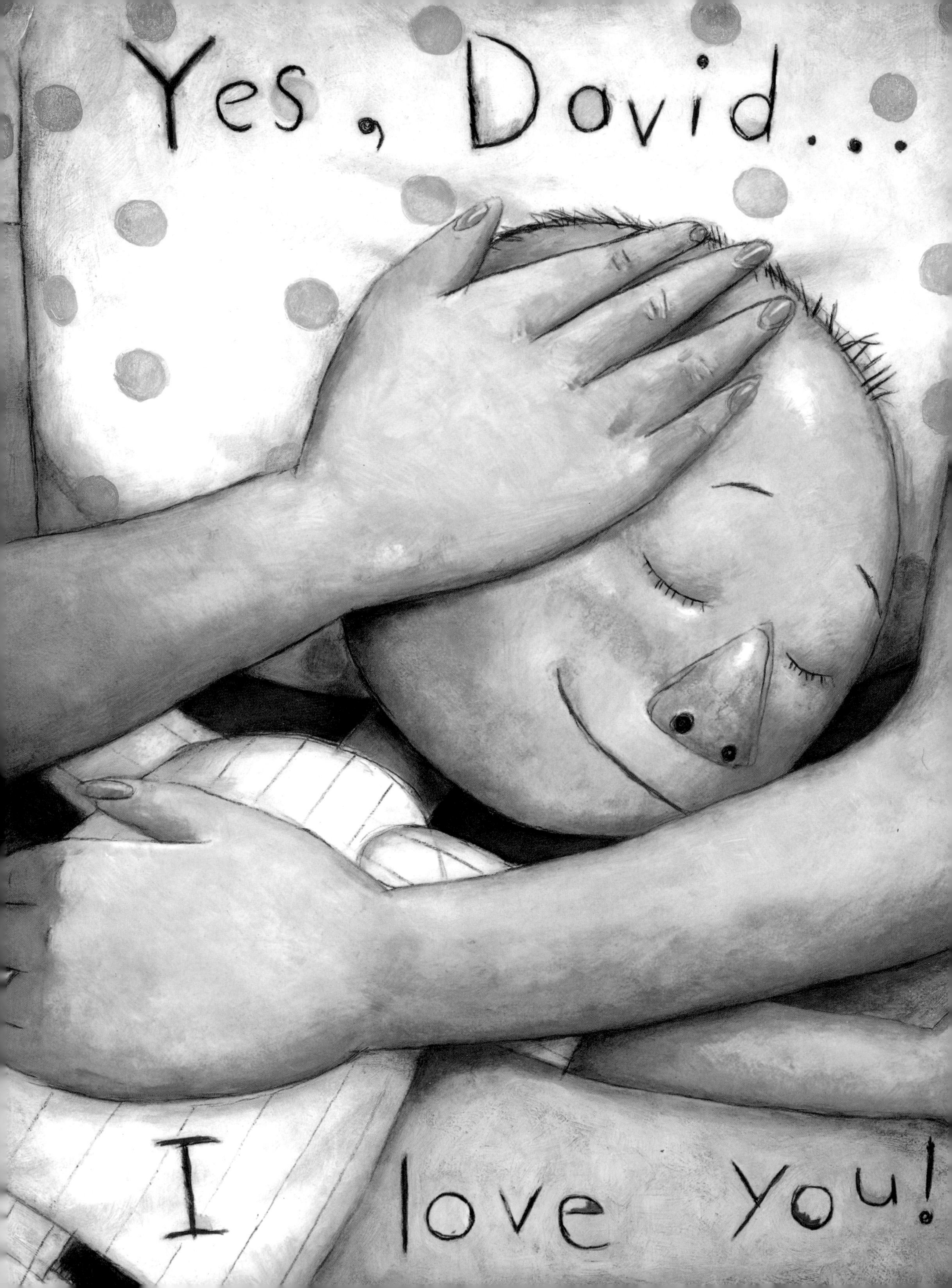
Yes, David...
I love you!